PHARMACY
IN THE
FOREST

HOW MEDICINES ARE FOUND IN THE NATURAL WORLD

THE FOREST

BY FRED POWLEDGE

Atheneum Books for Young Readers

TO TABITHA, MY FAVORITE HEALER

Atheneum Books for Young Readers

An imprint of Simon & Schuster Children's Publishing Division

1230 Avenue of the Americas   New York, New York 10020

Book design by Patti Ratchford

The text of this book is set in Apollo

First Edition

Printed in Hong Kong   10 9 8 7 6 5 4 3 2 1

Library of Congress Cataloging-in-Publication Data

Powledge, Fred.

Pharmacy in the forest: how medicines are found in the natural world / by Fred Powledge. — 1st ed. p.   cm.

Summary: Identifies medicinal plants and their natural habitats while also explaining how

these plants are found and tested for medical value.

ISBN 0-689-80863-1

1. Pharmacognosy—Juvenile literature. 2. Medicinal plants—Juvenile literature. [1. Medicinal plants. 2. Drugs.] I. Title.

RS160.P69   1998 615'.321—dc21 97-6938   CIP   AC

PHOTO CREDITS:

National Cancer Institute: 2, 35, 39, 40.

© Fred Powledge: 5-8, 10, 22, 25-27, 31-34, 36.

© Russell Mittermeier/Conservation International: 3, 9, 13, 15-18, 29, 42-43.

Agricultural Research Service, USDA: 24. U.S. National Arboretum: 5, 20, 26.

Editor's note: **Terms found in the glossary are in italics the first time they appear in the text.**

AUTHOR'S NOTE

Keeping up with all the plants that serve as medicines can be a confusing
task. Part of the confusion is that people in one part of the world may have a name for a
particular plant that is totally different from the name given to that same plant by people
in another part of the world. Science long ago realized the need for a
system of identifying plants so that scientists could communicate with each other.
The result was that plants (and animals, too) have been given scientific names as well
as common names. The common names are the names used in everyday
discussions about plants. There may be purple coneflowers blooming in your yard. A
scientist would know the plant by its Latin name—*Echinacea purpurea*. So would any
other scientist in the world, even in places where the common name is different.
That's why you will see both common and scientific names to identify
many of the plants.

WHERE DOES MEDICINE COME FROM?

Maryland pharmacist Ed Kerns fills a prescription the "modern," developed-country way.

The local drugstore? The pharmacy that's part of the huge discount store on the highway?

When you go to the doctor because you're not feeling well, she might give you medicines directly, or write a *prescription* that will be filled by a *pharmacist* behind a counter with plastic bottles with strange labels. Or, if the medicine doesn't require a doctor's prescription, you or your parents may buy it yourselves, carefully choosing from the great variety of bottles, boxes, and other colorful packages that fill the shelves of a pharmacy, discount store, or even the supermarket. Here, you can get aspirin for a headache, an antihistamine for allergies, or something for your poison ivy. All these, along with the *compounds* that the pharmacist fills under your doctor's direction, are medicines, and they all come from a store, right?

Well, right and wrong. Just as milk may come in a carton from the grocery store but really comes from a cow, medicines don't just come from a store, or even from a company that employs technicians in white laboratory jackets to make pills, capsules, creams, and syrups. Many of the substances that we use to cure our medical problems, ease our pain, keep us healthy—and in some cases even keep us alive—come from forests. They start out in the leaves, seeds, and roots of small flowering plants, or the bark or fruit of tall trees or the vines that cling to them, or even as microscopic *organisms*.

People have found their medicines in the forest ever since they first discovered plants, which was a very long time ago. Indeed, for most of the time we humans have spent on Earth, our medicine *had* to come from the forest, or at least from the natural world. The only pharmaceutical laboratory around was the one provided by nature.

According to the World Health Organization, plants and other natural products still play a major role in the health care of eight out of every ten people alive today. Many, if not most, of these people live in the less-developed countries of the world, most of which are situated in Latin America, Africa, and parts of Asia. In these places, income is lower and rates of poverty and hunger are higher. There are fewer of the facilities that many of us take for granted: highways, telephones, electricity, a dependable and safe water supply, education for everyone. Many of these countries are in the wide band of Earth that lies north and south of the equator between imaginary lines called the Tropic of Cancer and the Tropic of Capricorn. The short name for these countries is *the tropics*.

Tradition is one reason why people in the less-developed areas of the world rely heavily on the forest for their medicines. Some countries, such as China and India, have long histories of using plants for medicines. In China, perhaps 1 billion people use medicines based on plants. That's nine out of every ten residents of rural China, and four out of every ten city

Customers at this Chinese store in Washington, D.C., have a choice when purchasing herbs for medicinal use. On this side of the room, they can buy herbs by the ounce or pound. The drawers, like the glass jars, hold loose plant material.

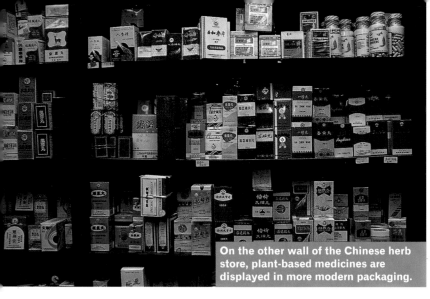
On the other wall of the Chinese herb store, plant-based medicines are displayed in more modern packaging.

dwellers. South Asia, which includes India, is the home of more than 1 billion people, some 800 million of whom rely on plant medicines. Another reason is that many people in those countries have less money to spend on medical care. Millions of the world's citizens manage to live on the equivalent of less than a dollar a day. They simply cannot afford to buy medicine from a store.

Natural products are important even in the health of the developed areas of the world. Each year, doctors in the United States write about 500 million prescriptions, one in every four of which is for a drug that started out as a leafy plant. More than half of all the drugs used by doctors and hospitals originated in the natural world. Of the world's twenty-five best-selling pharmaceutical products, twelve come from natural products.

And there are more where those came from. Experts say there are hundreds of thousands of plants, insects, and other organisms in the tropical forests that have never been studied by the world's scientists. As of 1995, flowering plants from forests in the tropics had already produced more than forty-five major pharmaceutical drugs. Researchers estimate there are seven times as many such drugs hidden somewhere in the forests, just waiting to be found.

They may not have to wait much longer. For many years, the developed world forgot its long history of relying on the plants of the forest for its medicines. We were using human-made chemicals in all parts of our lives—for creating plastics, for adding to foods, even for making the clothes we wear. We forgot about the natural origins of much that we use. But recently we have begun to pay more attention to the environment around us. We have begun to remember the great value of plants. We are rediscovering the pharmacy in the forest.

IT'S NOT JUST THE RAIN FOREST

When we think of the rich plant life in "the forest," we sometimes think of the tropical rain forest—perhaps the Amazon, the huge river valley in South America. The Amazon and the other rain forests of the tropics lie in a part of the world where there's plentiful rainfall (but also many rivers to drain the land and keep it from staying too soggy) and plenty of warmth and light. These are qualities that encourage rapid plant growth. Trees grow tall and thick, and the plants beneath them use the sunlight that reaches the ground to reproduce and spread so thickly, it all becomes a "jungle," a word from India that means a place so thick with vegetation that people cannot walk through it. Until recently, only small groups of humans lived in these forests. The trees and plants weren't cut down to make way for highways, factories, and homes. And those who *did* live there depended on the rain forest for their food and shelter, and their numbers were smaller. So they had less impact on these wonderful places.

The tropical rain forest remains the place where most of Earth's plant *biodiversity*, or variety of life, may be found. But it is not the only place where we find plants that are useful for medicines. There are other kinds of tropical forests, including dry ones (where the rainfall is much less); coastal ones (which are greatly influenced by the saltwater environment); and even cloud forests (which exist on hills and mountains so high, they are above the clouds much of the time). The first North Americans, the Indians, found medicinal plants in a place that most people wouldn't call a forest at all—the dry desert lands of the American Southwest.

Biodiversity thrives, too, in your own backyard, if you have one. Plants that are useful to humans can and do grow in the smallest city parks, or even in window boxes. The rain forest in the tropics is the place where plant life is the richest and most diverse, but the forests and woodlands of the cooler, drier parts of the world have given us many valuable plants, including some that we use to treat our most deadly diseases, such as *cancer*.

THE ROSY PERIWINKLE AND OTHER SAVIORS

The list of plants, herbs, and trees that have been and are useful to humans is a long one. Natural products are used in prescriptions and other medicines that cure or reduce the effects of many ailments, such as: • **malaria**, a disease that is transmitted by infected mosquitoes • **glaucoma**, an eye disease that is caused by too much fluid within the eyeball • **inflammation**, which is the redness, swelling, and pain that is the body's reaction to an injury • **heart disease** • **diarrhea** and • **nasal congestion**, which is the feeling of stuffiness that can come from colds and allergies.

There are many success stories of medicines from plants. The best one is that of the rosy periwinkle, a flowering plant that is both beautiful and a lifesaver. The plant's Latin name is *Vinca rosea*. It once thrived on the large island of Madagascar, which lies off the southeast coast of Africa in the Indian Ocean. Most of Madagascar is in the tropics and has a reputation as the home of many different sorts of interesting plants.

Residents of Madascagar knew the rosy periwinkle as a useful treatment for diabetes, a disease of people whose bodies don't produce an adequate amount of a substance called insulin. Employees of an American-based pharmaceutical firm, Eli Lilly, heard of the plant's reputation and conducted tests on it. Ely Lilly's scientists found that *extracts* taken from the periwinkle were not very effective against diabetes, but they did notice that the chemicals lowered the number of white cells in the blood.

White blood cells, which are also called leukocytes, are the body's defending armies. Whenever an infection threatens the body, white blood cells rush to the defense. A higher than usual number of white cells in a person's blood, therefore, is a sign of infection. An abnormally high number of white cells indicates leukemia, the name for a number of forms of cancer of the blood-producing tissues of the body. Leukemia is one of the cancers that affects children.

The good news was that there was a drug (one of the chemicals in the rosy periwinkle) that could lower the number of white cells in a patient's blood. This meant that the patient's infection was losing its battle against the body. After a lot of laboratory work, the Eli Lilly company isolated the chemicals that were doing the work. These are named vinblastine and vincristine, and they are part of the amazing group of substances called *alkaloids*. Now the two drugs are helping to keep people alive who ordinarily might have died. They are used in treating childhood leukemia and Hodgkin's disease, another form of cancer.

The bad news, for Madagascar, at least, was that the country that produced this marvelous plant was never properly rewarded for it. When the medicinal benefits of the rosy periwinkle were proven, Eli Lilly and Company suddenly needed large quantities of the shrub. So the company started growing its own rosy periwinkles, in neat rows on farmland near McAllen, Texas. Eli Lilly is believed to receive $100 million each year from sales of drugs based on the periwinkle. Madagascar has never received any compensation for its gift to the children of the world, and the country remains one of the poorest on Earth.

WHO FINDS THE MEDICINES IN THE FOREST?

The discovery of *Vinca rosea*'s value as a medicine is an exciting one. But it is only one of many. Scientists estimate that there are perhaps 250,000 plant *species* on Earth, and modern researchers have studied only a few of them for possible use as medicines. But that doesn't mean *someone* hasn't been studying plants, trees, and vines. For thousands of years, people all over the world have been finding, trying out, and using the pharmacy that lives in nature. In some of those places, such as China and India, careful written records have been kept of this exploration, testing, and use. In other places, where written language is not used, information about medicinal plants has been handed down from generation to generation by word of mouth. Only now is the developed world starting to appreciate the great contribution that has been made by these verbal record keepers.

For centuries, it was the people who lived in the forests themselves who searched for nature's medicines. Plants and other creatures always have been part of their everyday lives, just as automobiles, cornflakes, and television are part of ours. Being humans, forest people are curious about their surroundings. They experiment with what they find around them. (Have you ever tried out a new brand of cornflakes?) In most of these communities, it is the wise elders who do much of the searching. Just as important is the fact that they also do the remembering about what works and what doesn't.

Often the people who look after such information—these living libraries—are known as "medicine men" or "medicine women," or "shamans," or "healers." They exist in many societies, especially those of Indian communities in the Amazon rain forest.

The shaman is called a "magician" by some members of the community because they believe he is able to communicate with a mysterious other world and to perform feats that are not easily explained. He

Kwamasamoetoe, a village in Suriname, in tropical South America. It is the home of Okomayana Indians.

also is a healer, the person you see when you're sick, or when you've cut yourself on a thorn, or after you've been bitten by a snake. In many communities, the shaman serves as the group's religious leader.

Shamans and the work they perform may seem far removed from the everyday lives of people in the developed, industrialized world. But for hundreds of years, they have occupied important positions in the societies of native peoples, from the Arctic to the Amazon, from Siberia to America's Southwest. They are the doctors who have discovered many of the medicinal plants on which our own medicine is based.

How do the shamans get this very special knowledge? One way is by consuming plants or mixtures of plants in order to bring on the visions that, they and their communities believe, connect them to the spiritual world. For them, it is the spiritual world that is the home of sickness and death—and therefore the place where they can get *information* about sickness and death. These shamans feel that the visions help them to determine what is wrong with a tribe member who is sick, and to figure out what the treatment should be.

There are many vision-producing plants in the forests, especially those in the tropics. They are called hallucinogens, after the drugs they contain. These drugs can make the user think that he or she is seeing colors and designs that "never existed" before, or feel as if he is entering the body and mind of an animal, or somehow possesses great wisdom. Science tells us this is caused by the chemicals' effects on the human mind, and when the chemicals' effects wear off, the human is left with the same old colors, still outside the animal, with as much or as little wisdom as before, and quite possibly with a big headache.

But sometimes these drugs can play permanent tricks on the human mind, and leave lasting emotional damage. Or they can cause the user to do things (such as try to fly from a tall building) that result in serious injury or death. For those reasons, such drugs are outlawed in most developed countries.

There's as much difference as night and day between the shamans' use of vision-producing plants and a young person's use of such drugs to "get high." For one thing, the shaman knows what he's doing: Hallucinogenic plants have been a tradition in his community for hundreds, perhaps thousands, of years. The shaman isn't stupid. You certainly can't say the same about a young person (or an older one) who experiments with a drug that someone handed her on the street or at a party.

A healer in Suriname (left) prepares a plant mixture to treat fever.
We see the patient (right) receiving the treatment.

PEOPLE AND PLANTS

Many scientists from the developed world are fascinated by the plants that grow in the rain forest. Others are just as interested in the healers and shamans and the communities they lead.

Mark Plotkin is an ethnobotanist, one of a small but growing group of scientists who feel that it's difficult to understand plants without also understanding the people who use them, and vice versa. "Ethno" comes from the Greek term for "nation," and it refers to groups of people who are classified by their race, nationality, or other similarities. A botanist is someone who studies botany, the branch of biology that looks at plant life.

He explains his mission to preserve the forest world this way: "People have to realize, whether they're students, kids, scientists, or whatever, that it's not just a question of protecting plants or animals. People are part of the equation, too."

Through hundreds of years, people who live in the forests have learned which plants are dangerous and which are helpful in curing illnesses and lessening pain. Through trial and error and other means, they have found how much of a plant ingredient helps and how much of it hurts. They have also learned how to mix differ-

Scientists, just back from a collecting excursion in Suriname, lay out their botanical samples on the floor of a home in Asinolohopo village.

Ethnobotanist Mark Plotkin consults with a Yanomami Indian in Venezuela.

ent plant ingredients together to make other medicines that may be even more effective. It is the shamans who keep all this valuable information in their heads, and teach it to succeeding generations.

Scientists in modern laboratories may think that they can create the same medicines with book learning, test tubes, and human-made chemicals, says Mark Plotkin, but there's no real substitute for what is called "indigenous knowledge," the knowledge that is retained and handed down by the dwellers of the forest, often not in writing but in spoken words.

"Let me give you an example," he said not long ago. "I'm working on a new potion that's used in the Amazon forest to treat diabetes. It's incredibly effective. It consists of a mixture of four or five plants. Now, if you took the 80,000 species of plants in the Amazon and tested them one at a time, you *might* find a chemical in one of those plants that could duplicate this effect. However, first of all, a lot of this stuff depends on the dosage, which means that if you test 100 micrograms it might show no effect—or a toxic effect—whereas if you test 25 milligrams, which is what the shaman uses, you would get the right effect.

"The other complication is that this is a mixture of several different plants. So how many combinations of four or five can you come up with in 80,000 plants? And then you've got to worry about the dosage. It can't be done."

For an idea of how difficult it would be for a scientist or anybody else to test all those possi-

A healer drips latex from a cut vine into the eye of a glaucoma patient.

bilities, here's the number of five-plant combinations that could be made with 80,000 plants: **27,303,253,482,700,000,000,000.**

That's 27 sextillion, 303 quintillion possible combinations and then some. If it were possible to conduct one test per hour (and it isn't; such tests take years), you'd have quite a job on your hands: It would take more than 3 quintillion years, not counting time out for sleep, meals, and homework.

How was it possible for the forest people to come up with the right combinations themselves?

"Trial and error plays a major part," says Mark Plotkin. "But the shamans claim that a lot of this is done through the other world, through the hallucinogenic plants that give them the ability to peer into the chemical nature of these plants in ways that we just can't understand. That may sound like nonsense to us, but it seems to work for them in many cases."

Mark Plotkin has spent much time in the Amazon, visiting with shamans and learning their work. Does he believe the "other world" explanation? He recalled that some modern inventions and discoveries came about because their discoverers stumbled on important answers while they were dreaming. When this happens in the developed world, he said, the discoverers are called "geniuses." "When shamans dream about such things," he says, "we call it 'mumbo jumbo.' We don't understand it, so we dismiss it. But if it works, who cares?"

EXPERIMENTATION

Centuries of experience have taught the shamans not only which plants to use in order to get the results they want, but also how much of them to use. This is an important lesson—perhaps the most important of all when dealing with medicine (or, for that matter, anything else you put into your body). It applies equally to a bottle of aspirin that you purchase at a corner store or to a drug that has a reputation in the rain forest for turning its users into jaguars (briefly, and only in their minds): *Too much of anything will surely harm you. Different doses have different results.*

Anything can be toxic if we take too much of it, or if it conflicts in some way with our body's normal operation. Some medicines that are very helpful for one person might be quite harmful for another.

It takes a lot of serious study to know enough about chemicals so that we feel safe taking them into our bodies. Experiments, by their very nature, sometimes fail. Scientists who have worked for decades with plants and medicine sometimes get very sick when they experiment. Many substances we think of as medicines are also poisons. The difference often lies in how much of the substance you use. Because young people weigh much less than adults, their bodies react to lower doses of medicines, and so they are in even more danger. The obvious solution to this problem is this: Don't do it. Read up on the pharmacy in the forest, and daydream about someday becoming a scientist and a collector, an explorer of the Amazon or the forests of America's Pacific Northwest or of the Blue Ridge. Dream about being the researcher who finds, in a tiny flower that no one else noticed, a cure for *AIDS* or the common cold. But in the meantime, it's foolish and dangerous to experiment.

TOO MUCH OF A GOOD THING

Practically everybody swallows some aspirin every now and then. Aspirin is the world's most widely used drug and can be bought almost anywhere: in drugstores, supermarkets, even gasoline stations. Aspirin is considered to be an extremely safe drug. It's even used for babies, in a special baby-sized dose. Aspirin originally came from the leaves of willow trees, and people have been using it for 2,300 years.

The developed world started turning aspirin's chemicals into convenient, easy-to-swallow pills in 1899. It's good for headaches and muscle aches, helps make you feel better when you have a cold (we haven't found a medicine yet that'll make the cold go away, though), and even has been found to reduce some people's chances of having a stroke, which is damage to the brain that results from blockage in the blood supply. The usual dose of aspirin for adults is two tablets, with water, every four hours, with a maximum dosage of twelve tablets a day. (As with all medicines sold in the developed world, the recommended dosage is explained on the label, along with other helpful information.)

Aspirin, then, is good stuff. But not too much aspirin. If you gobbled down a whole bottleful of aspirin, you might be in serious trouble. Too much aspirin can damage the lining of the stomach or cause other problems. You would be poisoned.

There's another important thing to remember: Medicine that helps one person might hurt another. Your doctor might tell you not to take aspirin at all. For instance, if you're a child or teenager who has chicken pox, or the flu, taking aspirin puts you at risk of getting a rare disease known as **Reye's** syndrome, which can lead to seizures, paralysis, double vision, or a coma.

These warnings are present on every bottle of the wonder drug from nature, aspirin. They were *not* available 2,300 years ago when the Greek physician Hippocrates advised people to chew willow leaves to relieve their pain. Most people who followed Hippocrates's advice no doubt were happy that their pain was reduced. But some—those who chewed far too many leaves, or those whose bodies reacted badly to the leaves' ingredients—may not have fared so well.

A WORLDWIDE SAMPLING OF MEDICINAL WONDER PLANTS

Foxglove. Foxglove, an ornamental plant brought to the United States from Europe, graduated from wildflower to medicine two centuries ago. A British physician named William Withering visited a patient with dropsy—an affliction that left its victims with chests full of fluid and swollen bellies. The doctor discovered that unlike other dropsy sufferers, this patient was getting better. Dr. Withering found that on her own the woman was taking a mixture of more than twenty herbs and plants. He examined the mixture and concluded that it was foxglove that was making the difference. The herb has been an important part of medicine ever since.

Later, scientists determined that foxglove (*Digitalis purpurea* in Britain and *Digitalis ianata* in Europe) contains chemicals that improve the heart's circulation of blood. It causes the heart's muscle to produce a slower but stronger heartbeat. In William Withering's patient, that increased circulation was helping to remove the body's excess fluids, which were causing the swelling. Today, foxglove provides two of the world's most important heart medicines: digitoxin and digoxin.

According to one estimate, American doctors write more than 18 million prescriptions for foxglove extracts each year, and millions of people are alive because of the plant. All the medicinal substances are obtained from dried leaves of the plant. Until 1944, all the foxglove used in the United States was gathered by collectors in the forests and fields of Oregon and Wisconsin. After that, a company began growing the plant in fields in Oley, Pennsylvania, and experimented with different methods of drying the collected leaves. The result was a medicine that was much stronger than the wild version.

Ephedra. This substance is a perfect example of the dangers of experimentation. Ephedra, also called ma huang (and a member of the genus Ephedra), has been used in China for five thousand years. It is employed in India and China as a treatment for bronchial asthma. Similar substances are included in an estimated two hundred drugstore remedies in the developed world. The best known of these is pseudoephedrine (Sudafed®), which is used by millions of people for relieving the symptoms of colds and congestion in the nose. So ephedra and its cousins are very helpful.

They also can be very dangerous. Ephedra and related compounds increase *blood pressure*. They also speed up the heart rate and can cause palpitations, or strong throbbing of the heart. They can cause nervousness and dizziness and make a person nauseated. They can be a real danger for people who have high blood pressure (50 million Americans do), or diabetes, or thyroid disease.

Unfortunately, these dangers are hardly ever mentioned by companies that want to sell compounds containing ephedra as a substance that makes you feel good or helps you lose weight. (These mixtures are usually sold in "natural food" stores or in variety stores, but not in real pharmacies.) In 1996, several people became sick or died after taking such compounds that they had purchased. Many of them were young people who thought they were buying legal herbs that would give them the same feelings as illegal ones. Such drugs are sometimes referred to as "recreational drugs," but for these victims, the result was anything but recreation.

Neem. In India, the neem tree *(Azadirachta indica)* is such a valuable plant for humans that it has been called "the village pharmacy." In addition to providing inexpensive medicines for generations of people in Asia, the tree produces chemicals that are helpful for repelling insects; it is used to make soaps and waxes; and it's an excellent way to reforest land where the trees have been cut down.

Although neem's safety when it is directly consumed by humans is uncertain, the tree and substances from it are widely used medicines. These include its oil, primarily, but also its fruits, seeds, leaves, and bark. Many people use neem as a fungicide, meaning it destroys harmful fungi such as athlete's foot and ringworm, and as an agent that kills harmful *bacteria,* such as those that cause food poisoning, blood poisoning, boils, abscesses, and typhoid. It may be useful in preventing (but not curing) *virus* diseases. People use neem to get rid of head lice, to treat malaria, to reduce pain and fever, and for family planning.

As if that weren't enough, neem is a toothbrush. Millions of people in Africa and India snap twigs off neem trees and use them to clean their teeth and keep their gums healthy. Where else can you get your bath soap, insect repellent, painkiller, and shade all in one place, and keep your teeth clean in the bargain!

Ginseng. Some forest medicines are little known to most people in the developed world, or even to city dwellers in the countries where they are found. This isn't the case with ginseng, an herb that is so well known and popular that in the forests of the eastern United States it has been classified as an endangered species.

The wrinkled root of Panax ginseng, which sometimes resembles the body of a human with stubby arms and legs, has been used for a long time in Asia by people who wish to make their interest in sex stronger (a substance that does this, or is believed to do this, is called an aphrodisiac). There is no scientific proof that this is true. But the root has an even wider use: People all over the world consume it, in capsules, powders, and teas, to give their bodies strength against *stress*. There is some scientific evidence that ginseng does, in fact, strengthen the body and help it to resist disease.

There is a problem with ginseng's popularity: As more and more people have started collecting the herb, both for their own use and for sale to others, they have begun to dig up practically all the ginseng there is. Authorities have had to pass laws setting up an official season for collecting, so that ginseng plants get a chance to grow and reproduce themselves. And as more and more people have purchased the herb in stores that sell such products, some sellers have cheated. They have sold products labeled "ginseng" that contain no ginseng at all.

Purple coneflower. This is one of the names for a handsome wild-flower named *Echinacea*. It is a relative of the daisy, with drooping purple petals surrounding a ball-shaped head full of seeds that are beloved by hungry birds. The plant is a native of the United States, where the Indians long ago discovered its values as a drug. Today, parts of the flower are ingested for treatment of colds and sore throats and to build up the body's resistance to infections, or applied to the skin to help heal wounds. The flowers are also quite beautiful, and in the fall when their petals and seeds have dried they become attractive again. Birds arrive and perch on the end of each plant's long stem and sway back and forth while they peck away at their seed dinner.

Serpent-tooth plant. Like many of the medicines of the forest, this one has several names. "East Indian snakeroot" is one of them. Scientists know the plant as Rauvolfia serpentina. A substance in its dried root, *Rauwolfia serpentina,* is well known to medical science as a *tranquilizer* and as a drug for lowering blood pressure. The drug is known to the medical world as reserpine.

The plant, which is from Asia and has relatives in Africa, was the world's first tranquilizer; that is, it calms the human's central nervous system. It is of great importance in helping people who suffer from the severe mental disorder known as schizophrenia. It is equally important for millions of others who have high blood pressure; it brings down the pressure and smoothes out the heartbeat. In the United States alone, doctors write more than 22 million prescriptions every year for reserpine.

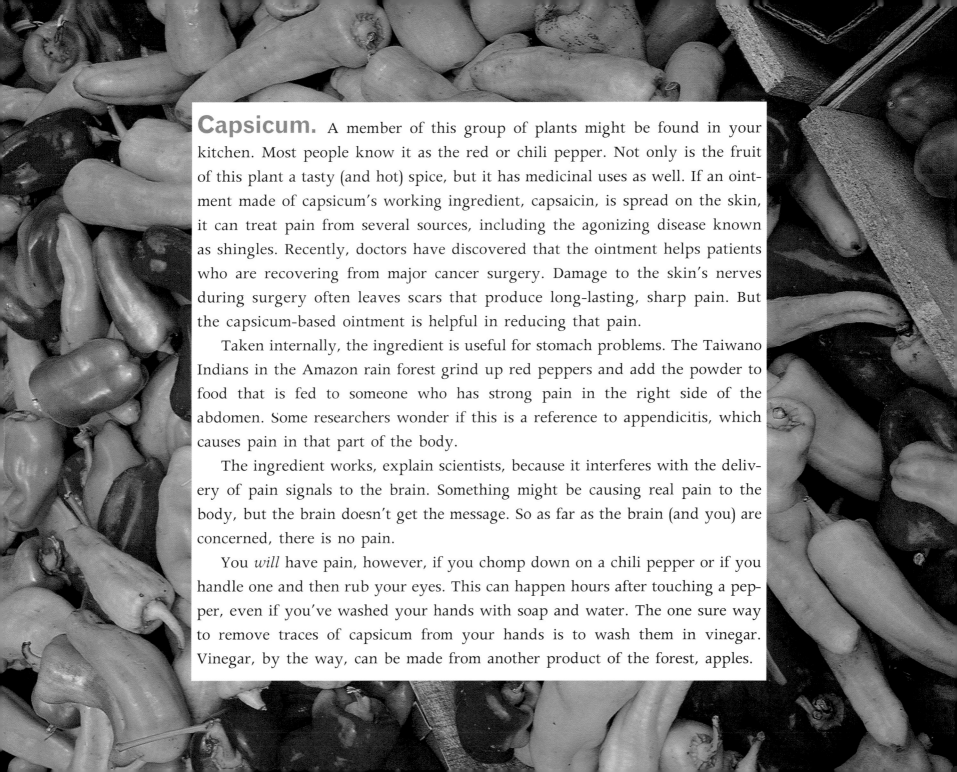

Capsicum. A member of this group of plants might be found in your kitchen. Most people know it as the red or chili pepper. Not only is the fruit of this plant a tasty (and hot) spice, but it has medicinal uses as well. If an ointment made of capsicum's working ingredient, capsaicin, is spread on the skin, it can treat pain from several sources, including the agonizing disease known as shingles. Recently, doctors have discovered that the ointment helps patients who are recovering from major cancer surgery. Damage to the skin's nerves during surgery often leaves scars that produce long-lasting, sharp pain. But the capsicum-based ointment is helpful in reducing that pain.

Taken internally, the ingredient is useful for stomach problems. The Taiwano Indians in the Amazon rain forest grind up red peppers and add the powder to food that is fed to someone who has strong pain in the right side of the abdomen. Some researchers wonder if this is a reference to appendicitis, which causes pain in that part of the body.

The ingredient works, explain scientists, because it interferes with the delivery of pain signals to the brain. Something might be causing real pain to the body, but the brain doesn't get the message. So as far as the brain (and you) are concerned, there is no pain.

You *will* have pain, however, if you chomp down on a chili pepper or if you handle one and then rub your eyes. This can happen hours after touching a pepper, even if you've washed your hands with soap and water. The one sure way to remove traces of capsicum from your hands is to wash them in vinegar. Vinegar, by the way, can be made from another product of the forest, apples.

PLANTS UNFAMILIAR TO THE DEVELOPED WORLD

Many of the plants, trees, and shrubs that live in the pharmacy of the forest are familiar, or at least their names are, to people in the developed world. But there are hundreds, even thousands, of other plants that are known only by their scientific names, or by the names given to them by small Indian tribes that live in remote parts of the tropical rain forest. These are important parts of the pharmacy in the forest, too.

In the Amazon, people use the twigs of a tree known as *arbusto* to fight fever, the bark of *carapanauba* for ulcers, tea made from *pedra unica* for diabetes, and *xixuaxa* for rheumatism. The *Annona* family includes a multipurpose medicine. The family produces edible fruit (cherimoya is known as the "ice-cream fruit" because it tastes like a delicious sherbet), and Amazonian Indians have a number of uses for the tree. They make a tea of the leaves to produce a diuretic drink to relieve swollen feet. In stronger doses, Annona serves as a general tonic for the body. Medicine men from the Taiwano tribe in eastern Colombia make a tea from the leaves of a related tree, *Xylopia*, and use it to treat people who have had "a great fright," which is called *susto*. Elsewhere the tea is used to help people get to sleep.

As is the case with many forest plants that are used by indigenous people to treat health problems, science in the developed world has not yet caught up and begun testing all the medical possibilities. But all that is changing now.

If you've seen many movies about the Amazon and the people who live there, you may have heard about *curare*—the poison that native people apply to the points of their arrows and blowgun darts when they are hunting fish, animals, and birds. Actually, there are several curares (the word comes from an

A Tirio Indian boy from Suriname aims an arrow at a fish dinner. Many Indian communities in the rain forests use mixtures of plant chemicals to make poisons, called curare, that will kill or stun their quarry.

Indian name for "poison"). They are made from the bark and stems of several plants, mixed together in a precise recipe. Each Indian tribe that uses arrow poisons has its own favorite plant and method of preparing the poison. Hunters use different curares for hunting different foods.

Often the bark is removed from the plants, mixed with other ingredients, boiled in water, and then strained. Then it is evaporated (over fire or in sunlight) until a paste or syrup forms. It is this paste that is placed on the points of arrows or darts. When an arrow or dart finds its mark, the ingredients in the curare enter the victim's bloodstream and produce paralysis. In some cases, the poison only stuns the game long enough for the hunter to arrive on the scene.

Richard Evans Schultes and Robert F. Raffauf, who wrote about their Amazon studies, say that in most tribes, the medicine man who is in charge of the curare mixtures "usually has elaborate formulas, frequently calling for up to fifteen or more plants . . ."

Sir Walter Raleigh, who explored the North American east coast for England, knew about curares as early as 1595, when he took a sample home to England. But it was many years later that medical science started using some of curare's ingredients in the operating room—to relax a patient's muscles during surgery.

NOT JUST PLANTS

Medicines don't come just from leafy plants. Insects contain substances that are of interest to science as possible medicinal substances. So do fungi, which are plants that lack roots, leaves, and stems. Fungi also lack the ability that green plants have to use sunlight to make food energy. Our best-known fungi are mushrooms, but they also include the mold that forms on stale bread and the fungus that causes athlete's foot. The molds have been especially useful to medicine. They produced penicillin, a group of *antibiotics* that people use to treat bacterial infections. Before penicillin, a tooth infection or a cut with a rusty nail might lead to a long, painful illness, or could even be fatal. Now that we have this inexpensive drug, there is less chance of even a mild fever.

Scientists are only now beginning to seriously search for medicines in bacteria, those one-celled creatures that are so small, we see them only under microscopes. Another place that future medicines may be found is the bottom of the sea. In recent years, deep-sea researchers have discovered strange vents, or holes, at the bottom of the deepest oceans. Warm water flows from these vents into the otherwise cold ocean, and in that warmth grow creatures that humans have never seen before. Some of them may contain compounds useful to medicine.

Molds occur anywhere, even in your kitchen. Here they grow (left and center) on a bell pepper and (right) on a slice of bread.

LOOKING FOR A CURE

If you live in the Western Amazon, or in southern India, or any of dozens of other places in the world, you probably already are taking advantage of the pharmacy in the forest. A shaman or a traditional healer, or a wise and experienced family member, may know just the thing (be it leaf, seed, bark, or root) to relieve the headache that refuses to go away, or the fever that's causing your parents to hover about your bed, sleeping pad, or hammock with worried looks on their faces.

But many of us *don't* live in those places. We live in the industrialized world, where medicine mostly comes in a bottle or a capsule, and where decisions about which medicines we should take are made by professional people who have spent many years in special schools and training in hospitals.

How do the plants of the forest become useful in the world of corner pharmacies, hospitals, and doctors in white jackets? And, especially, how can they help in the struggle against two of our most feared diseases—cancer and AIDS?

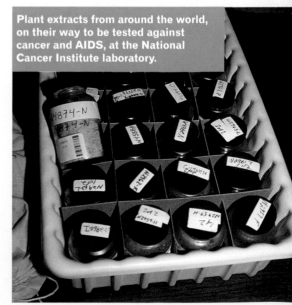

Plant extracts from around the world, on their way to be tested against cancer and AIDS, at the National Cancer Institute laboratory.

They must be tested, in a process that is lengthy, expensive, and more often than not, ends in disappointment. Companies that make drugs do some of the tests, for they are always hoping to discover new drugs that will bring in money. In the United States, the federal government does testing, too.

The federal program is operated by the National Cancer Institute, or NCI, a part of the agency known as the Department of Health and Human Services.

Gordon M. Cragg is the friendly, helpful chief of NCI's Natural Products Branch. As its name implies, this group of scientists collects plants and other natural products from around the world (particularly in the tropical countries)

NCI's Dan Danner inspects frozen plant material. The walk-in freezer is -20 degrees Celsius, but Danner wears shorts because it's summertime.

and tests them for possible medicinal use against cancer and AIDS. They also collect all sorts of creatures from the sea. The National Cancer Institute has been in existence since 1937, but the Natural Products Branch has been around for only ten years. At first, Dr. Cragg and his fellow workers examined only the plant material that was collected for them by another federal agency, the U.S. Department of Agriculture (USDA). That agency sent in some 35,000 samples of plants, most of them from the *temperate zones* and a few from the tropics. More recently, NCI has hired other institutions (the Missouri Botanical Garden, New York Botanical Garden, and the University of Chicago) to do the collecting. These organizations have concentrated on the less-developed countries of the tropics—Central and South America, Africa, Madagascar, Southeast Asia. In close to forty years, NCI has removed an estimated 400,000 chemicals from organisms its collectors have sent in, and has tested those chemicals for possible use against cancer and AIDS.

NCI's testing process starts out at an ordinary-looking warehouse with some not-very-ordinary-looking machines inside it. The machines are large, walk-in freezers, where fruit, seeds, bark, twigs, and other plant parts from around the world are stored at -20 degrees Celsius, until they are ready for testing. From the moment the plants are collected in the field, they are placed in plastic bags that have bar codes—the same thick and thin black lines that you see on a box of cereal and everything else in a supermarket. The codes stand for unique numbers, which NCI's computers can read at any step of the testing process. The identifying numbers, along with all the information that NCI's scientists gather about the specimen and the chemicals it contains, are stored in large computer data bases. So the entire life history of the source—and its performance in tests against cancer or AIDS—can be obtained on a computer screen in a matter of seconds.

When the laboratory is ready to test a natural product, the product is ground up until it becomes a powder. For the bark of some trees, this requires a piece of machinery that noisily tumbles, tears, and rips the wood apart. For marine organisms, a different machine is required: a restaurant-sized hamburger grinder! Scientists freeze these marine creatures on shipboard shortly after their nets bring them in. Then they send them, still frozen hard as rocks, to NCI. Lab workers then chip away with hammers and chisels to get pieces small enough to feed through the grinder. The result is something that looks like a very light-colored burger. You probably wouldn't want to eat it.

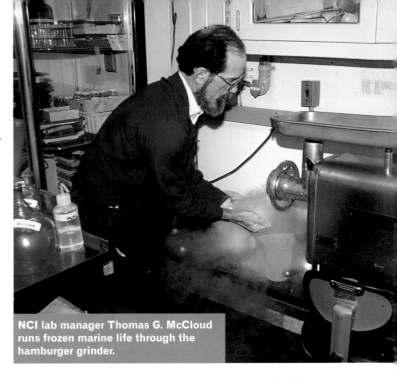

NCI lab manager Thomas G. McCloud runs frozen marine life through the hamburger grinder.

After this point, a natural product loses its regular identity and becomes, instead, two new bar-coded numbers, one for each of the methods that will be used to test the substance. "Think of it as a library book," said Dr. Cragg. "The librarian checks the book in and out by its bar-coded number."

Researchers remove the chemicals that make up the plant by soaking samples of the plant in water and in a solvent, then drying the results. What's left is called the crude extract. It is this extract that will be tested as a possible anticancer and anti-AIDS agent.

In the room where the cancer testing takes place, there are stacks and stacks of small, rectangular, clear plastic plates, each with ninety-six dimples—called "wells"—in them. Each well contains a sample of human cancer cells in a substance that is dyed pink. NCI has a collection of sixty such "human cancer cell lines," as they are called, representing seven basic cancers of humans, including those of the lung, colon, brain, kidney, skin, ovaries, and blood.

Scientists add tiny, precisely measured doses of the plant or marine extract to each of the wells, and wait to see what happens. In most tests, there is no change. But in some, there may be a change in the pink color. This means that the extract (from the plant or marine organism) is having an effect on the cancer. It is either killing the cancer or it is slowing down the cancer's growth. Either way, the scientists start paying special attention to that extract. There's still a long way to go, though.

"Our next objective," said Dr. Cragg, "is to try to isolate the single chemical that's doing this from the mixture in the extract." If the NCI scientists are lucky, it will be just one of the plant's many chemicals that is acting against the cancer. But sometimes it's several chemicals, working together. Sorting that out, of course, is much more complicated.

In some respects, the tests used by high-tech modern science to find new medicines involve as much trial and error as what the "unscientific" shaman experiences in the forest. Lab workers divide the extract into a number of groups and test each group, repeating the process until they have narrowed things down to the chemical or chemicals that attack the disease. All this can take four or five months, or as much as two years. "And once you've done it for cancer, you go through the same process to test it against AIDS," said Dr. Cragg.

If the lab finds the chemical it's looking for, it is tested again—this time in laboratory mice who have been infected with cancer. If the chemical successfully attacks the cancer in the mouse, that's the signal for even wider testing, this time in rats, dogs, and other laboratory animals. Researchers are looking for signs that the chemical will eliminate or slow down the cancer, of course, but they also are looking for trouble. By giving the

Extracts of plant substances float in jars at the **NCI** laboratory.

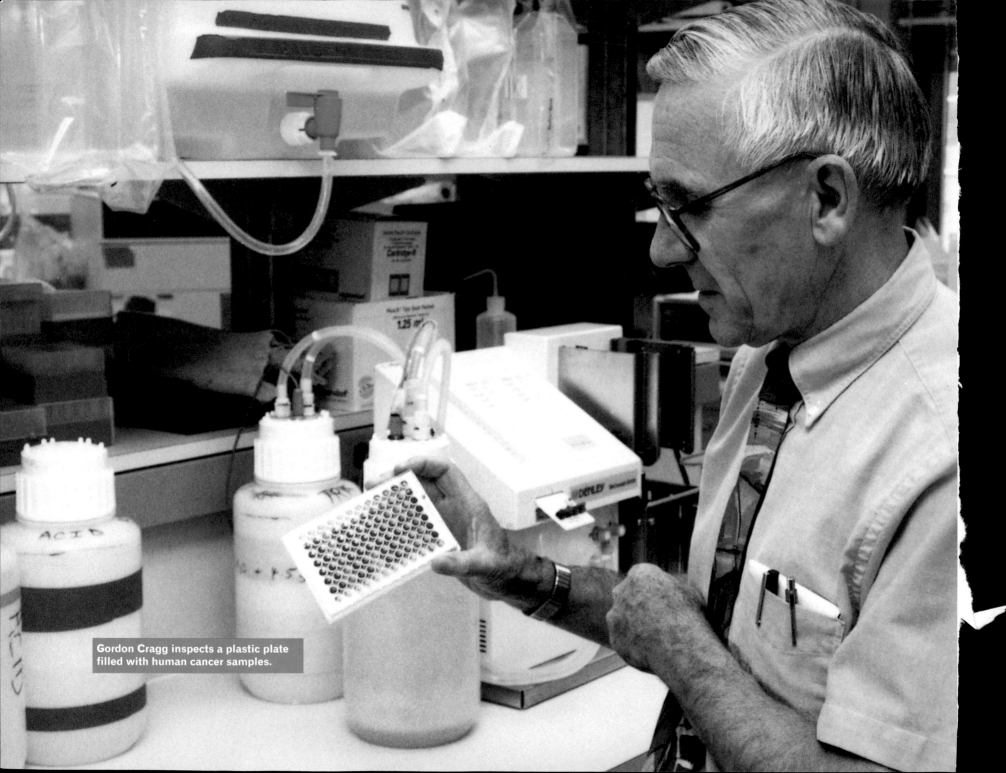

Gordon Cragg inspects a plastic plate filled with human cancer samples.

lab animals larger and larger doses, the NCI scientists are trying to find out how much of the chemical will cause more harm than good—or, in their language, what the chemical's *toxicity level* is. If the level is high, meaning the animals are easily poisoned by the extract, the chemical will be sent back to the deep freeze. But if it isn't, the next step will involve human beings.

In the clinical trials, scientists try out the chemical on real people who are suffering from the diseases. In the early phases, these people are volunteers who have serious cases of cancer or AIDS. They have reached "a certain level of desperation," said Dr. Cragg. "They are eager to try anything that might prolong their lives."

One aim of the early testing in humans is to get an idea of the maximum dosage of the chemical that will do its work in people without harming them. Once that information has been collected, the chemical is tested in people who are suffering from as many as thirty different kinds of cancer, as well as in healthy volunteers.

Only the chemicals that make it through this long and tough process go to the next step: designation as a new drug by another federal agency, the Food and Drug Administration (FDA). Even then, the work of NCI's researchers is far from done. They must figure out the best ways to package the drug—should it be injected by needle, or taken as a pill or capsule?—and to make it available to the people who need it. They must find large sources of the plant that produces the drug, because it usually takes many plants to make even a tiny amount of medicine.

The entire process is like a funnel: Thousands of plants enter the wide top of the funnel at the beginning, and scientists start to examine each one of them as possible drugs in the fight against humankind's worst diseases. The funnel narrows, though, as plants fail the test. Finally, at the small end of the funnel, a handful of plants emerge as the useful drugs of tomorrow. Dr. Cragg estimates that, in the case of an anticancer drug, the chances are about one in forty thousand or more. In addition, the process takes a great deal of time—from ten to twenty years.

"It's not a high return," says Gordon Cragg. "But the thing is, when you come up with it, it's right."

FROM TRASH TO TREASURE

The rosy periwinkle is one superstar among our medicines that originate in the forest. Another is taxol, which comes from the Pacific yew *(Taxus brevifolia)*, a not-very-beautiful, shrubby-looking plant that foresters, in their search for sources of valuable lumber, considered a "trash tree," or one that had no value. Now we know that *Taxus brevifolia* produces a proven medicine for fighting cancer. It has kept many people alive who otherwise would have died.

Taxol sounds like what some people call a "magic bullet"—a scientific discovery that immediately and completely cures a big problem. There have been a few such big events in the history of the world. One was the discovery that certain molds (which are created by fungi) can contain the antibiotics called penicillin. Another was the invention of a vaccination against smallpox.

In reality, magic bullets don't just come out of nowhere and fall into a scientist's hands. The big breakthroughs in medical science are almost always the result of a lot of hard, painstaking, and sometimes disappointing work by a lot of people. That was certainly the story with taxol. The drug was almost abandoned twice before the world accepted it as the magic bullet it is.

There were stories that the early American Indians used the needles of the yew tree to treat lung ailments, but modern researchers paid little attention to this, dismissing it as "folk medicine." In the testing program that ran from 1960 until 1982, plant collectors from the U.S. Department of Agriculture explored the temperate world, gathering bits of bark, seeds, stems, roots, leaves, and flowers. Their samples went to the National Cancer Institute. Among those early samples was a bit of the yew.

Two years later, tests showed that something in the yew seemed to be effective against some cancers. Not until 1969, though, did NCI know that the substance was taxol. They tested it against one form of cancer in mice, but it didn't perform particularly well. So taxol went on the shelf (or rather into the deep freeze), along with thousands of other bits of leaf, root, stem, and bark that showed little promise.

Then, in the late 1970s, NCI started using a more refined testing method and tried taxol again. This time the chemical showed activity against cancers of the breast in mice as well as melanomas, which are particularly dangerous skin cancers. It slowed down their destructive growth, or stopped the growth entirely. The scientists at NCI began to look at taxol more closely, and by the early 1980s, the government chemists were ready to test the drug on humans.

At first, there were serious problems. Several of the patients with cancer who volunteered for the tests died when they were poisoned by taxol. It seemed that the amount of taxol that was necessary to do the *good* work of defeating cancer was also doing the *bad* work of poisoning the patient. Some scientists wanted to abandon the drug right then, for the second time.

One scientist, however, changed the method of administering the drug so that it was taken into the body slowly. This caused less of a shock for the body. The volunteers were not poisoned.

In 1988, other researchers noticed that taxol was remarkably effective against cancer of the ovaries, which kills an estimated 14,800 women every year in the United States. And still other scientists found evidence that taxol was also useful against several other forms of cancer, including breast cancer. About

forty thousand people die every year in the United States from this disease.

All of a sudden, the demand for taxol from researchers conducting tests shot up. The National Cancer Institute, which not long before had been about to abandon taxol, now had a new problem: how to find enough of the drug. The best source of taxol was the bark of the Pacific yew tree. But removing a tree's bark kills it just as surely as removing your skin would kill you.

Lots of people and organizations went to work solving the supply problem. NCI entered into an agreement with a pharmaceutical company, Bristol-Myers Squibb, to search for other sources of taxol and to manufacture the drug. Researchers in France figured out a way to extract a chemical from a yew tree's needles, and not just from its bark, that could be used to make taxol. This was a very important discovery. A tree's needles return every year; they are renewable. Bark isn't. A forestry company, Weyerhaeuser, started growing *Taxus brevifolia* in neat rows on tree farms in Washington State.

In the span of twenty-six years, taxol had gone from a "trash tree" to a wonder drug. The medicinal version made by Bristol-Myers Squibb now costs thousands of dollars for a cancer patient's treatment. The pharmaceutical company refers to taxol as its own product, without mentioning the fact that many government and university scientists developed the chemical, and that the taxpayers of the United States paid for the research.

WHAT ABOUT TOMORROW?

All of Earth's people once depended on plants—trees, flowering plants, herbs, shrubs, vines—for their medicines. Billions of them still do. Even the developed world, which in past years has drifted away from the pharmacy in the forest, is rediscovering the wonderful, useful medicines that grow in the wild.

But what will happen if "the wild" becomes no longer wild? If the forest disappears? It is happening right now. More and more people are crowding onto Earth, and each of them needs room to live, food to eat, a place to work. Farmers need land to grow the food with which to feed all the new people. There are estimates that Earth's population will almost double by the year 2030 from the number that lived here in 1990. (After that, say the experts, the population growth will slow down.) That means that if you were five years old in 1990, by the time you're thirty or forty or forty-five, you'll be sharing the planet with more people than you ever imagined.

How can the world's population continue to grow without destroying the environment that provides a home to medicinal plants? A lot of people are hard at work trying to answer that question. We have learned in recent years that the tropics, especially the rain forests, contain huge amounts of plant, animal, bird, and insect life that we've never even known about or studied before. We have also learned that the tropical forest may *look* like a tough, dense jungle in some places, but really is a fragile place. A small bit of change—like a highway cut through the forest—can disrupt the delicate balance of animals and plants and their environment and lead to their destruction. What is destroyed might have been the flower or tree that could treat our most serious diseases, like cancer—or our most ordinary ones,

In Madagascar, whose forests gave the world the miraculous rosy periwinkle, the environment is rapidly being destroyed. This land used to be rain forest. The trees were removed so cattle could graze and rice could be grown. Now the soil is eroded and little will grow.

like the common cold. Because of exactly this kind of change, much of Madagascar, which gave the world the rosy periwinkle, and so gave millions of children and adults their lives back, has lost much of its forests and the plants and animals that grew there.

Many of those who study the forests say that we must be careful to protect more than the plants, birds, bugs, and animals. We must also protect the people who live in the forest. In the places where the plant life is richest (and where we in the developed world know the least), healing knowledge resides in the minds of the people: the shamans, the medicine men and women. They are the vital connection between the world of nature and the world of health. Keeping their home in the forest healthy keeps *them* healthy. And they and their forests may help to keep the rest of us alive and healthy, too.

Not all useful medicines come from tropical forests. The forests of the temperate world are the homes, too, of herbs, shrubs, and trees that reduce our pain, keep us healthy, and even make us live longer. *All* kinds of forests need protection. It's not just the tropical forests that are threatened. Acid rain from industry in the American Midwest damages trees in the Appalachian and Adirondack Mountains, and unrestrained logging in temperate forests of the Pacific Northwest and the Great Lakes region has severely damaged them and the plant and animal life they hold. It's great to wear T-shirts that say SAVE THE RAIN FOREST, but we shouldn't neglect the other forests, either.

Those people who favor the development of forests into what they consider more useful places (such as farms, housing, or industrial sites) make the argument that there are so many creatures remaining on

Burning is the favored way to clear forests for conversion to agriculture. But what important medicines are lost in the flames? Here, a baobab forest burns in Madagascar.

Earth, it won't matter if we cause the extinction of a few plants or animals by cutting down a forest.

But others feel very strongly that it *does* matter a great deal. For one thing, a plant that may seem useless or even troublesome today may be a treasure tomorrow. Taxol is one example of that. For another thing, we humans have a responsibility to nurture all the other forms of life with which we share our planet.

Russell A. Mittermeier, who is the president of one of the most important American-based environmental groups, Conservation International, suspects that there are 100 million or more different kinds of creatures on Earth—animals, bugs, plants, things that live in the sea. Dr. Mittermeier thinks every bit of it is worth protecting.

"After all is said and done," he said not long ago, "this is still the only planet where we know for sure that life exists. As far as we know, we are still unique in the entire universe. And we, as living creatures ourselves, not only depend on other forms of life for our own survival; we also have a moral obligation to maintain other forms of life."

He also thinks humans have an obligation to learn a lot more about the organisms around them. In a society where technology rules, where we can send spacecraft into the solar system and build an "information superhighway" for computers, we don't have very much knowledge about how many other forms of life share our planet.

Fortunately, scientists and nonscientists alike are reawakening to the great value of the organisms with which we share our planet. A rediscovery of Earth is going on, and the pharmacy in the forest is but one part of it.

GLOSSARY

AIDS. AIDS (acquired immunodeficiency syndrome) is a fatal disease in humans. It is caused by a virus that can break down the body's immune system, which normally gives it the strength to fight off infections. The disease is spread from person to person by sexual activity or by the exchange of body fluids, such as the blood of the infected person with the blood of the other (this can happen when drug users share hypodermic needles). There is no vaccine yet to prevent AIDS, as there is for such diseases as polio and smallpox. There is also no cure, although some of the newest treatments do seem to slow down its progress.

Alkaloid. An alkaloid is a substance that contains the element nitrogen, along with carbon, hydrogen, and often oxygen. Alkaloids are found in many plants. They can be poisonous (as is the case with nicotine, which is in tobacco, and strychnine, a rat killer that comes from the seeds of a tree), and they can be medicinal (as in quinine, a treatment for malaria, and morphine, for pain relief). Perhaps the most commonly used alkaloid is caffeine, which is present in coffee, many soft drinks, and cocoa. Most arrow poisons are alkaloids.

Antibiotic. An antibiotic is a medicine that is usually made from microorganisms (creatures so tiny that humans can see them only with the help of a microscope) that attack other, "bad" microorganisms, such as bacteria that cause infection. Penicillin is perhaps the best-known antibiotic. Because some antibiotics are harmful to certain organisms but harmless to others, there are several of them, each developed for a specific use.

Bacteria. Bacteria are one-celled organisms that are so small they can be seen only with a microscope. Some are helpful to humans, and some are harmful. Some can grow only with oxygen around them, some can grow only in an environment with no oxygen, and some can survive either way. We would be in big trouble if we didn't share the planet with bacteria that decompose waste or assist in the process known as photosynthesis. On the other hand, we'd be better off without the bacteria that bring us tetanus, typhoid fever, and cholera.

Biodiversity, or biological diversity. This term refers to the great variety of all life on Earth. Earth's inhabitants—humans, smaller animals, microscopic organisms, insects, plants, water creatures, and everything else—are very different from each other. Not only are people different from tomatoes, but people are different from other people, and no two tomatoes are the same. Look at your parents, whose genes combined to put you on Earth: You may resemble one or both of them (people may say, "He has his father's chin," or, "She has her mother's eyes"), but you don't look exactly like either one. You (and they, and the tomato that looks like no other tomato) are part of the great diversity of our planet's environment. Many scientists and others fear that, with the continued destruction of forests, hillsides, and wetlands to make way for cities, farms, and highways, biological diversity is being lost at a much higher rate than ever before. That's troublesome, because it is in diversity that animals and plants contain the differing qualities that allow them to overcome disease and adapt to changing conditions. The term "biodiversity" is short for "biological diversity."

Blood pressure. This is the measurement of the pressure that our blood places on the walls of our arteries. It's usually measured by a device that encircles the arm. If the pressure is too high (a condition known as high blood pressure, or hypertension, and one that is shared by millions of Americans), we are in increased danger of having a stroke, in which brain tissue is destroyed because not enough blood is getting to it, or of severe damage to other organs, such as our kidneys.

Cancer. Cancer is the uncontrolled growth of the body's cells. Most cells do specific jobs in the body, but cancer cells have only one aim: to keep making more cells. They rob normal cells of the nutrients they need, and therefore starve them out. A group of cancer cells is called a tumor. Some cancers enter pathways in the body (the blood system is one) and spread to other parts of the body, while some remain in the tissue where they originated. Because cancer can be a deadly disease and one that can cause its victims great pain and suffering, much research is directed at finding treatments for it. Several medicinal plants have been used to treat cancer, and many others are being tested.

Compound. A combination of two or more ingredients. Few medicines consist of just one substance, but are mixtures of several chemicals.

Extract. A substance that is removed from another substance. Many medicines made from plants are made not from the entire plant but from its extracts. The act of removing the substance is called "extracting" it.

Organism. Any living plant or animal. Size doesn't matter; elephants are organisms, and so are microscopic bacteria.

Pharmacist. A person who is trained (usually at a specialized school) to make and sell drugs. The place where many people in the developed world go to purchase medicines is called a pharmacy. Although most of the drugs a pharmacist sells have been prescribed by doctors (see PRESCRIPTION), the pharmacist keeps track of other medicines his or her customers may be taking, so they may be warned about possible dangers of mixing medications. A pharmacist may work in a pharmacy, drugstore, or hospital or clinic.

Prescription. Usually a written note from a doctor to a pharmacist, authorizing the pharmacist to sell a certain drug to the doctor's patient and setting forth the dosage. Not all medicines require a doctor's prescription; those that the patient can find on the open shelves of a pharmacy or other store (like pain relievers and cold medications) are called *nonprescription* or *over-the-counter* drugs.

Species and classification. Earth has so many different inhabitants (see BIOLOGICAL DIVERSITY) that it's necessary that we classify everything just so we can keep track of it and know what to call it. The basic unit of classification is the species, which serves to identify plants, animals, or insects that have similar genes. Members of the same species successfully reproduce among themselves, but not with members of other species. Humans are a species, and so are pear trees.

Similar species are grouped into a genus; several genera are members of a family; several families make up an order; a group of orders forms a class; classes form a phylum (sometimes called a division); and at the top of the list is the kingdom. The two big kingdom categories are animals and plants. Just to make things even more complicated, some scientists maintain that there should be as many as five kingdoms, to take care of creatures such as fungi and bacteria. Here's an example of what science calls *classification,* starting at the top of one of the kingdoms and ending up somewhere closer to home:

Kingdom: Animalia (includes everything from coral reef sponges to earthworms to lobsters to spiders to crocodiles)
Phylum: Chordata (frogs, birds, mammals)
Class: Mammalia (bats, elephants, whales, primates)
Order: Primate (orangutans, tree shrews, humans)
Family: Hominidae (humans, past and present)
Genera: Homo (only one example at present)
Species: Homo sapiens sapiens (look in the mirror!)

Stress. When most people speak of "stress," they're talking about all the pressures that living is putting on them—the teacher's deadline for turning in a report, the strain of trying to make the soccer team. When they get older, it's the pressures of the job, or paying the bills, or having enough time to spend with the family. When a scientist talks about stress, it's something else. Stress is whatever happens from the outside that changes the body's usual internal chemistry. Not all stress is bad. The chemical changes brought on by exercise (bike riding, swimming, jogging) cause stress that is certainly "good," if you don't overdo it.

Stress also may be used to refer to the pressures placed on the environment by humans or other forces.

Temperate zones. The parts of the world that lie (on paper, at least) between the imaginary lines of the tropics (see TROPICS) and the Arctic Circle in the north or the Antarctic Circle in the south. As a rule, the climate is cooler in the northern and southern temperate zones than in the tropics. The sun is never directly overhead here, as it is in the tropics. Its angle differs between winter and summer, and there are distinct seasons. Most of the United States lies within the northern temperate zone, but parts—some of Alaska and all of Hawaii, Puerto Rico, and many Pacific islands—are outside.

Toxicity level. This is a way of measuring how harmful a compound, such as a medicine or a pesticide, is. "Harmful" is another way of saying "poisonous" or "toxic." Since practically everything on Earth is harmful if too much of it is consumed, science has developed ways to judge the degree of toxicity. One of them uses laboratory animals such as rats, mice, dogs, and rabbits. Increasingly large doses of the substance being tested are given to groups of test animals until half of a group—50 percent—are killed. That dosage is then called the "LD 50" dose, or the lethal dose for 50 percent. Researchers then calculate what this means for humans. They take the smallest LD 50 that killed animals in one of the test groups, multiply it by the weight of a human being, and that is the "human acute lethal dose," or ALD.

If all that sounds endlessly complicated, here's another way of looking at it: In converting what they have learned from animals to doses for humans, scientists build in a hundred-fold margin of safety. They assume that a healthy adult human is ten times more sensitive than an animal, and that young, old, and sick people are ten times more sensitive than healthy adults.

Tranquilizer. A drug that makes animals (including humans) calmer and more tranquil. Such drugs do their work by affecting the body's central nervous system (the brain and the spinal cord), which controls what the body does and how it responds to actions from outside. Many tranquilizers have been found in plants.

Tropics and tropical zone. The parts of the world that lie between two imaginary lines, called the Tropic of Capricorn and the Tropic of Cancer. Scientists "drew" these lines around Earth at twenty-three and one-half degrees south and north, respectively, of the equator, which is another imaginary line that runs around Earth's middle.

(The equator is at zero degrees, the North Pole is at ninety degrees north, and the South Pole is at ninety degrees south.) Why a figure like twenty-three and one-half degrees north and south? Those are the most northern and southern places on Earth where the sun appears directly overhead at noon. It does that on two days a year.

Virus. A virus is an organism so small that it can be seen only with a special device known as an electron microscope. At the stage of life where they are most bothersome, viruses don't behave like most other living organisms. Rather, they latch on to existing cells, eating their food and stealing their energy. Some viruses make their victim cells cancerous. Others cause mumps, measles, influenza, and the common cold. There's very little that can be done after a virus strikes except to follow the old rule: Get plenty of rest, drink lots of liquids, and wait. Vaccinations help prevent some of them from striking, however.

MAI

3-30-99